Origins

DIY Dinosaur

Nick Ward ✱ **Marina Pérez Luque**

OXFORD
UNIVERSITY PRESS

Miss Joy had an exciting project for her class.
"This weekend, I want you to make a model of your favourite animal," she said.

Freddie knew exactly what he was going to do. He loved dinosaurs, so he would make the best T. Rex model ever!

On Saturday, Freddie couldn't wait to get started. But he had football in the morning and shopping with Mum in the afternoon.

On Sunday, Freddie started his model. He found some plasticine. It was soft and easy to mould, but the legs kept going floppy — and then its head kept falling off!

When his model was finished, Freddie drew a prehistoric landscape on card. The dinosaur looked so real, you could almost hear it ROAR!

"I need a strong box to keep it safe," said Freddie, so he put the dinosaur on the sofa and went to find one.

Just then, his dad came in and sat down on the sofa without looking. Squish! He sat right on the dinosaur!

"Oh no!" cried Freddie. "It's as flat as a pancake!"

"I'm so sorry, Freddie," said his dad. "I'll help you make a new one."

Dad went and got a box from the garage. There were lots of tins, springs, bolts and bits of wood inside.

"We need to make the new dinosaur *really* strong," said Freddie.

Freddie gave his dad a block of wood.
"This could be the body," he said.
"And we can use this old ladle for the
head and the neck."

"I'll stick all the bits together with extra-strong glue," said Dad. "You can't do this, Freddie. You might stick your fingers together."

Freddie smiled. His dad had already got a scrap of newspaper stuck to the end of his nose!

Dad stuck the ladle on the block of wood. "Like this?" he asked.
"No, the other way round!" said Freddie with a sigh. "That's it!"

Little by little the T. Rex began to take shape. They added screws, an old sardine tin and more wood.

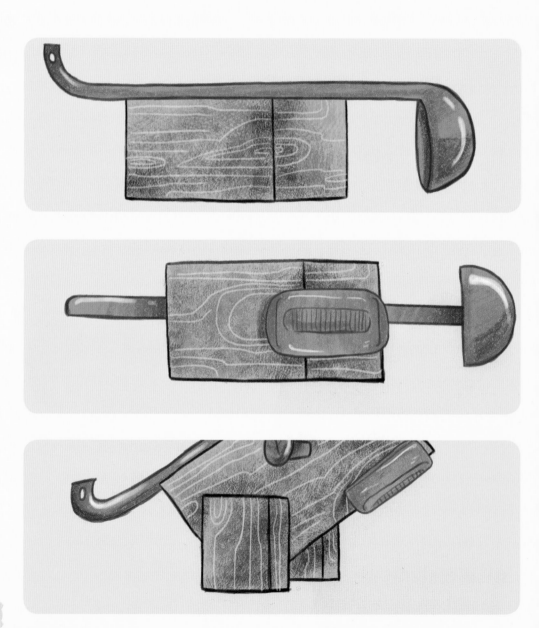

"It looks brilliant," said Dad.

"It needs painting," said Freddie.

"OK," said Dad. "You start painting and I'll get lunch ready."

Freddie painted his model green and yellow. He added eyes. When it was dry, he put it on the sofa.

Dad finished making lunch and flopped down on the sofa without looking again! "Watch out!" yelled Freddie, but he was too late.

"Aaargh!" roared Dad. He jumped up and stomped round the room in pain. "That dinosaur bit me!"

"Oh, Dad!" Freddie laughed. "At least you didn't squash it. But now you look just like a T. Rex yourself!"

Can you retell the story?

To find out more about the right stuff read ...

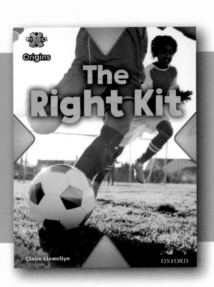

... and find out how Max, Cat and Tiger made a bird hide.